Are You My Best Friend?

Written by Cardelle Szego

Illustrated by Angela Gooliaff

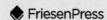 FriesenPress

One Printers Way
Altona, MB R0G 0B0
Canada

www.friesenpress.com

ISBN
978-1-03-912742-5 (Hardcover)
978-1-03-912741-8 (Paperback)
978-1-03-912743-2 (eBook)

1. JUVENILE FICTION, SOCIAL ISSUES, FRIENDSHIP

Distributed to the trade by The Ingram Book Company

on each page

you will find

the owl was there

the whole time

Deep in the forest, high up on a reed,
a dragonfly was born,
and she took off with great speed!

"I'm off to find my **best friend!**" she said.
"But where could he be? I know I'll find someone
out there for me." With a plan in her mind,
she began to take flight. "It's a big world
out there! Who knows who I might find!"

She flew all day and flew all night,
when suddenly a blue jay came into sight!

"Are you my best friend?!"
she yelled with delight.

The blue jay said, "Yes! For a time, I just might . . .
Follow me, I know a great spot! We'll head down
this path to the right, but I'd like to be alone
once the day turns to night."

"Well, that won't work," said the dragonfly.
"I want a best friend forever," she said with a sigh.
And with that, she was off in the blink of an eye.

She flew all day and flew all night,
when suddenly a koala came into sight!

"Are you my best friend?!"
she yelled with delight.

The koala said, "Friend? That is a big word, too
big for my like." Then suddenly, an idea popped
into his head. "Why don't you fly by my side,
but don't ever call me your friend."

"Well, that won't work," said the dragonfly.
"I want a best friend forever," she said with
a sigh. And with that, she was off
in the blink of an eye.

She flew all day and flew all night,
when suddenly a skunk came into sight!

"Are you my best friend?!" she yelled
with delight. "What?" said the skunk,
as he opened one eye.

"I was sleeping here just fine! I won't wake up
for you! For me, it's always nap time."

"Well, that won't work," said the dragonfly.
"I want a best friend forever," she said with
a sigh. And with that, she was off
in the blink of an eye.

She flew all day and flew all night,
when suddenly an alligator came into sight!

"Are you my **best friend?!**"
she yelled with delight.

The alligator said, "Well hello, little dragonfly!
You came at just the right time! I am hungry,
you see, and I think you will do just fine."

"Well, that won't work," said the dragonfly.
"I want a **best friend forever**," she said
with a sigh. And with that, she was off
in the blink of an eye.

She flew all day and flew all night,
when suddenly a fox came into sight!

 "Are you my **best friend?!**"
she yelled with delight.

"Oh, sure! said the fox. "In fact, meet the rest
of my friends, right here on my right! I have
hundreds, you know, I never travel with just one.
If you come with us, you'll have **tons of fun!**"

"Well, that won't work," said the dragonfly,
"I want a best friend forever," she said with a sigh.
And with that, she was off in the blink of an eye.

She flew all day and flew all night,
when suddenly a bear came into sight!

"Are you my best friend?!"
she yelled with delight.

The bear said, "I'll give you one day a week,
as long as you like. I spend all my days searching
for honey, so feel free to go fly, but don't tell the
other bears, because I am not a sharing guy.

"Well, that won't work," said the dragonfly.
"I want a best friend forever," she said with a sigh.
And with that, she was off in the blink of an eye.

She flew all day and flew all night,
when suddenly a sloth came into sight!

 "Are you my best friend?!"
she yelled with delight.

The sloth said, "Absolutely! But just so you know,
I have no interest in games, I do everything
slow. I enjoy being here, hanging upside down!
Wouldn't you say my coat is
the most beautiful brown?"

"Well, that won't work," said the dragonfly.
"I want a best friend forever," she said with a sigh.
And with that, she was off in the blink of an eye.

After many days and many nights,
the dragonfly began to feel like her plan
would never work out right.

She stopped for a break on a nearby tree;
she needed a rest from the flying, you see.
Then suddenly, she heard a noise from above:

"Hoot, hoot," went the animal,
and it sounded like love.

"Could that be my best friend?" she whispered to herself with delight. Then suddenly, she saw two eyes shining bright.

"Hello, Dragonfly, would you like to sit with me?
I saw you flying up above behind my tree.

Your wings caught my eye, the colors so bright,
I was wondering if you would like to
fly with me tonight?

"I have lived here awhile and always saw you speeding past, we could wander the woods together, and maybe then I will have found my best friend at last."

The dragonfly could **not believe** what she heard.

She was so busy, **flying in circles** all around,
she had no idea that this whole time, the owl
was sitting right here, **waiting to be found**.

After flying around for what seemed like forever,
here was her best friend, and she knew
that they belonged together.

CPSIA information can be obtained
at www.ICGtesting.com
Printed in the USA
BVHW022017250422
635321BV00002B/8